MW00949331

THE BEST BIRTHDAY CAKE IN THE HISTORY OF EVER!

A Christmas Tradition Celebrating the Birth of Jesus

WRITTEN BY:
JENNIFER A. HILL

WRITTEN BY:
MARY M. WALKER

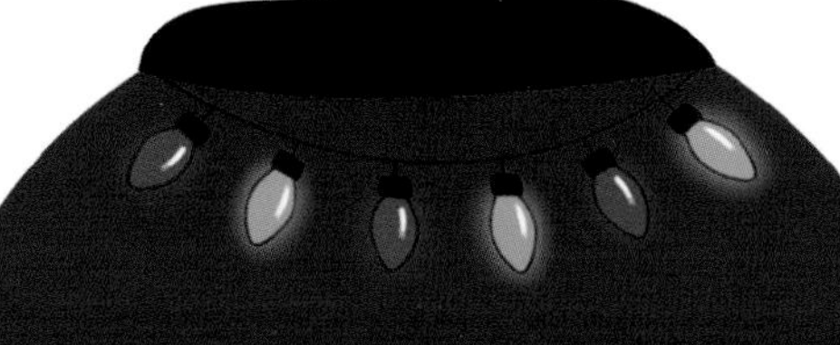

ILLUSTRATED BY:
KENZIE STRINGO

Our Mission

It is our mission to bring wholesome goodness back to the family table with stories that inspire TOGETHERNESS.

yada, yada, yada...

Written by: Jennifer A. Hill and Mary M. Walker

Cover Design by: Mary M. Walker

Illustrated by: Kenzie Stringo; assisted by Robin Muentes

Formatting by: Scott Neece, Kenzie Stringo & Mary M. Walker

Snapchat lenses by: Scott Neece

Bible Verses from the International Children's Bible

Published by: HBDJC Publishing, LLC

2700 Observation Trail

Rockwall, TX 75032

www.HistoryofEver.com

Contact us for wholesale opportunities.

Printed in the United States of America.

First Edition

ISBN: 978-1-7356480-0-2 (Hardcover)

ISBN: 978-1-7356480-1-9 (Digital Book)

For our kids

Hayes, Holt, Andrew, Maddie & Abbie

No one is YOU and that will always be your super power.

Download "Teddy the Dog" & "Teddy at Play" lenses on Snapchat!

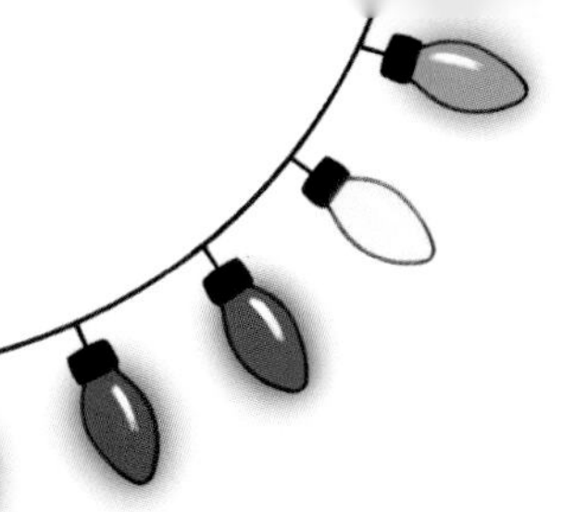

But wait, there's more!

Your book includes:

- Craft time & cake baking
- A Christmas traditions search & learn game
- Teddy the Dog's Fun Costume Changes
- The story of the birth of Jesus
- Recipe tied to Bible verses
- Certificate of cake completion
- Fun rhyming story

Visit our website to:

- Download a printable crown to decorate.
- Find crafts for the Star and Angel cake toppers.
- Access a convenient printable recipe.
- Get helpful hints to make your party a success!
- Check out our blog for fun stories, activities and crafts for the family!

www.HistoryofEver.com

Follow "Teddy the Dog" & Our Crew!

- @historyofever
- @historyofeverbooks
- "History Of Ever Books" Channel
- Download the "Teddy the Dog" and "Teddy at Play" Lenses on Snapchat

Check us out online & enter to win!

Hey guys! Guess what?
Christmas is here.
It's my favorite season,
full of laughter and cheer!

My name is Hayes!
I have a story to share
about family traditions
and the power of prayer.

These are my parents, they run our kit-n-caboodle.
There's me, my brother, Holt, and Teddy our Goldendoodle.

Mom and Dad taught me to pray many years ago.
No doubt they were right, most parents are, you know!
No matter the question, big or small, bring it to God, He can help with it all.

Now that you've met us, we're ready to start the story of celebration God put in my heart.

So sit back,

relax

and

enjoy.

This journey began when I was a boy.

It was sometime near the beginning of December.
I was listening to my teacher, like a good class member.

I learned of holiday traditions like Boxing Day and Kwanzaa,
and the differences between Christmas and Hanukkah.

Each celebration had become its own tradition.
This got me thinking and was the start of my mission!

We had our own
Christmas fun each year
with traditions we enjoyed
and still hold dear.

We loved caroling with cocoa on a fun carriage ride,

decorating our tree
and of course,
the ice slide!

When kids think about Christmas, SANTA is a big thing.
But the day is truly about the birth of a King.

I wanted to create
a family tradition
with a reason,

something that
celebrated Jesus
and His season.

But what could it be?
What could we do?
My mom suggested asking
God for a clue.

The very next morning
I jumped out of bed!
I ran to my parent's room...

FULL STEAM AHEAD!

I was super EXCITED!
I knew they'd be glad.
So I ran in and yelled...

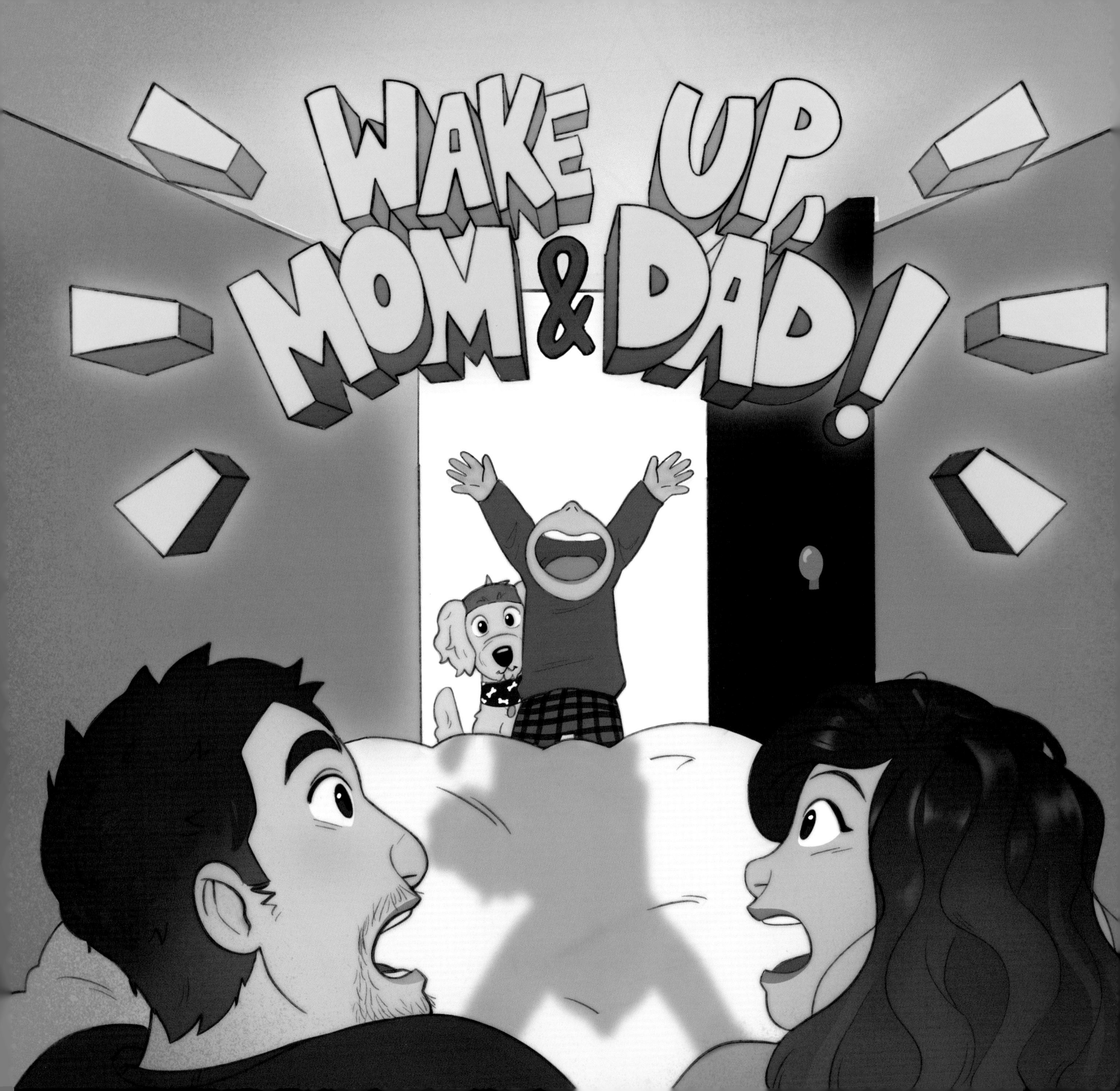
WAKE UP, MOM & DAD!

God answered my prayer!

You won't believe this...

WE'RE HAVING A
BIRTHDAY PARTY
FOR
JESUS!

Of course God would give me this idea full of fun.

After all, He's a dad who wants to celebrate His son.

We decided the party would be
Christmas Eve night.

Mom started working
on the perfect invite.

Making His birthday cake
would highlight the evening.

A recipe tied to scripture,
we then began weaving.

The day had arrived! All my best friends were there.
Dad gathered us together and we began with a prayer.

Before baking began, we had fun crafts to do.
We even made birthday crowns with construction paper and glue.

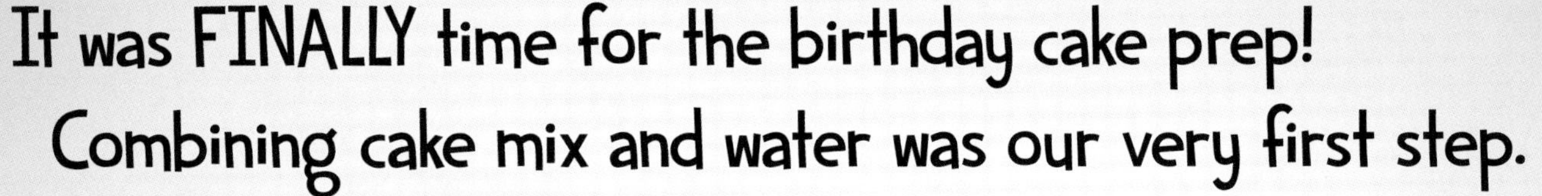

It was FINALLY time for the birthday cake prep!
Combining cake mix and water was our very first step.

The water symbolizes our belief in Jesus Christ.
By believing in Him, we've been given eternal lif

Bible Verse - John 4:14
But whoever drinks the water I give will never be thirsty again. The water I give will become a spring of water flowing inside him. It will give him eternal life.

We stirred the batter, it turned red like a heart!

Showing us the love Jesus gave from the start.

Mom read Romans 5:8. God showed us His love by sending his Son down from above.

Bible Verse - Romans 5:8
But Christ died for us while we were still sinners.
In this way God shows his great love for us.

Next, we stirred in chocolate chips
to represent the sin that comes from our lips.

Like the chocolate, our hearts can be dark and dim,
but our sins melt away when we believe in Him.

The batter was ready to pour in a pan.
Even the shape was part of the plan.

Dad said, "Our cake will be round with no beginning or end; like God's never-ending forgiveness, on which we can depend."

Bible Verse - 1 John 1:9
But if we confess our sins, he will forgive our sins. We can trust God. He does what is right. He will make us clean from all the wrongs we have done.

We moved to the living room while the cake was baking.
Mom created a station for cider and cocoa making.

Dad read Luke 2, the story of that momentous night
when Jesus was born and the world was made right.

Bible Verse - Luke 2:1-20
"The Birth of Jesus"
(Available at the back of the book)

Ding!

Mom presented the cake on a beautiful stand.
All the kids chanted "FROSTING!" in a loud demand!

The frosting was white, but we weren't sure why.
Then mom read Psalm 51:7 as we began to apply.

That scripture explained all we needed to know.
Jesus' love purifies and leaves our hearts white as snow.

Bible Verse - Psalm 51:7
Take away my sin, and I will be clean.
Wash me, and I will be whiter than snow.

The cake was now frosted
and looked really great!

Then Dad said, "Hold on kids,
we still need to decorate."

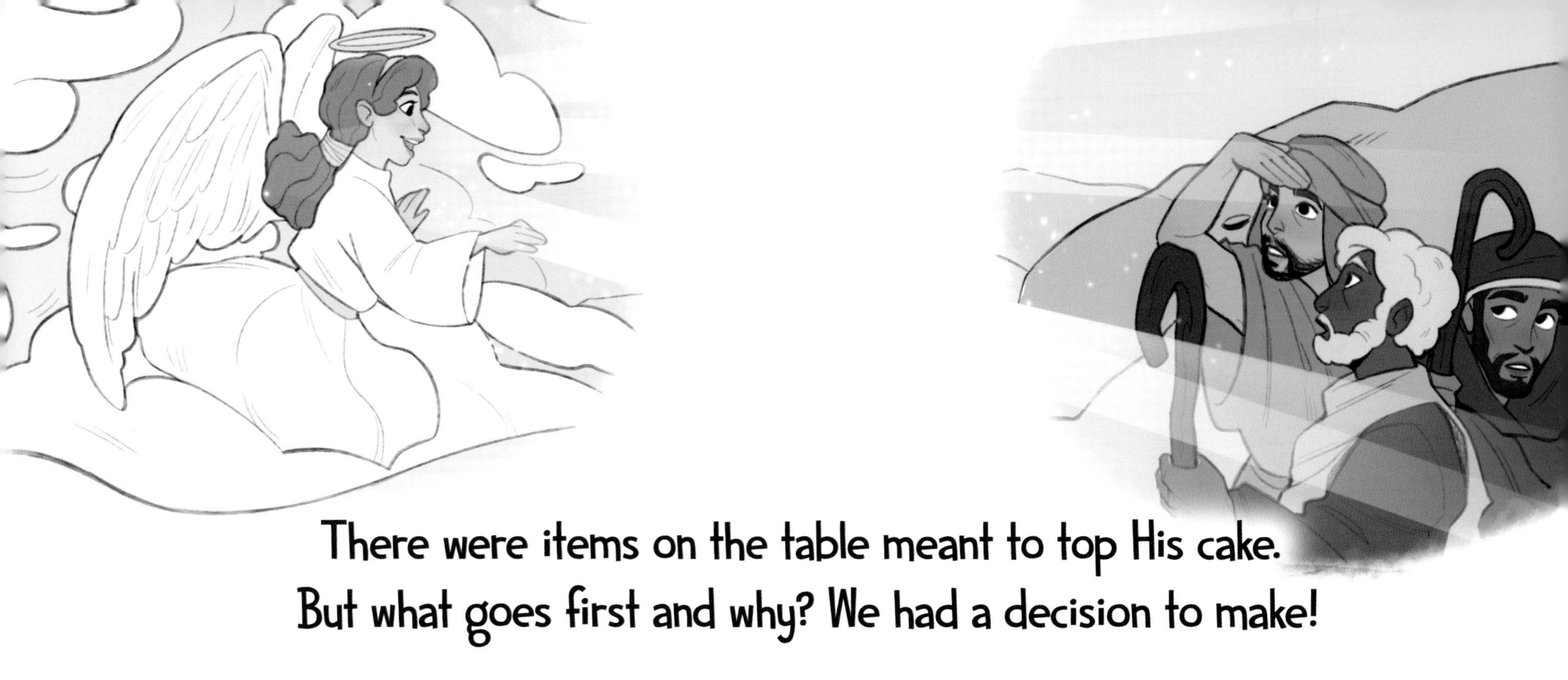

There were items on the table meant to top His cake.
But what goes first and why? We had a decision to make!

Mom said, "Luke 2:10 tells of an angel spreading joy
and announcing the birth of a special little boy."

A messenger sent from heaven to spread the good news?
The angel belonged in the middle, it was easy to choose.

Among the remaining toppings shined a gold star.
Could it be the one that led the wise men from afar?

Indeed the star was an important piece of the story.
It was the guiding light for others to witness God's glory.

Bible Verse - Matthew 2:9
The wise men heard the king and then left. They saw the same star they had seen in the east. It went before them until it stopped above the place where the child was.

Mom gave us evergreen stems to place at the base.
By accepting Christ as Lord, we forever grow in grace.

Bible Verse - 2 Peter 3:18
But grow in the grace and knowledge of our Lord and Savior Jesus Christ. Glory be to him now and forever! Amen.

Every birthday cake needs candles, I'm sure you agree!
Jesus is a King, so what kind should they be?
We thought purple candles
would display royalty best,
with twelve on the cake,
one for each month
we are blessed.
Bible Verse - Psalm 103:19
The Lord has set his throne in heaven.
And his kingdom rules over everything.

Lighting the candles was our final step.
Matthew 5:16 explains this in depth:

"Let your light shine for all to see,
so everyone will know your faith in Me."

Bible Verse - Matthew 5:16
In the same way, you should be a light for other people.
Live so that they will see the good things you do.
Live so that they will praise your Father in heaven.

It was time to sing the most important song.
Happy Birthday to Jesus! Even Teddy howled along.

Everyone had chills and felt the true Christmas spirit!
We sang so loud, we knew Jesus could hear it!

Then with one deep breath,
the candles were out.
His birth saved us,
we had no doubt.

It's been many years since
that prayer for a plan.
A favorite family tradition
from the night it began.

Each year as we prepare
His special birthday cake,
we remember the
sacrifice He chose to make.

I'm sure YOUR family will
create something clever
as you make
"The Best Birthday Cake in the History of Ever!"

Our journey is complete and I hope you did see...

This story was really never about me.

Happy Birthday, Jesus!

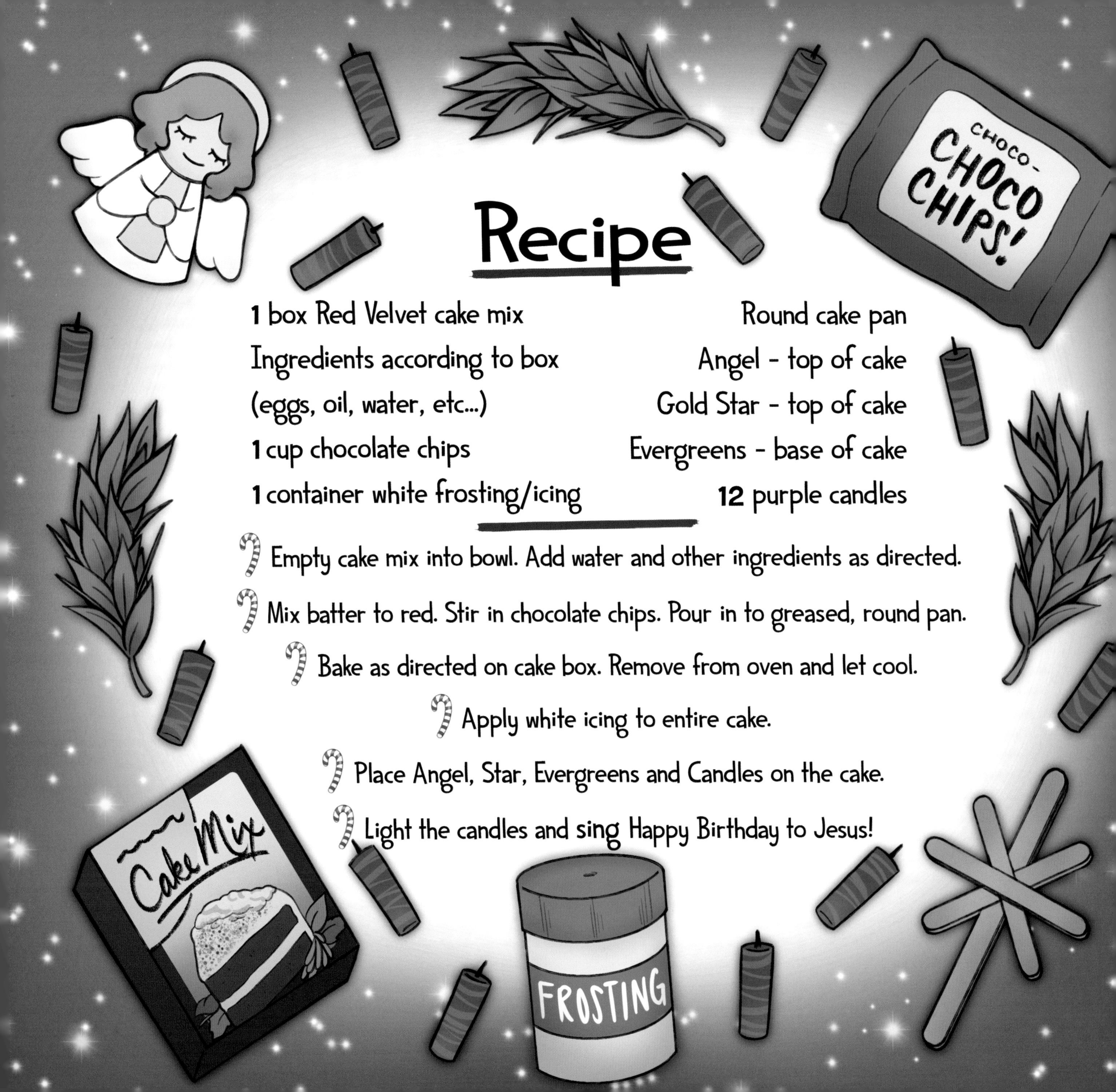

Recipe

1 box Red Velvet cake mix
Ingredients according to box
(eggs, oil, water, etc...)
1 cup chocolate chips
1 container white frosting/icing

Round cake pan
Angel - top of cake
Gold Star - top of cake
Evergreens - base of cake
12 purple candles

- Empty cake mix into bowl. Add water and other ingredients as directed.
- Mix batter to red. Stir in chocolate chips. Pour in to greased, round pan.
- Bake as directed on cake box. Remove from oven and let cool.
- Apply white icing to entire cake.
- Place Angel, Star, Evergreens and Candles on the cake.
- Light the candles and sing Happy Birthday to Jesus!

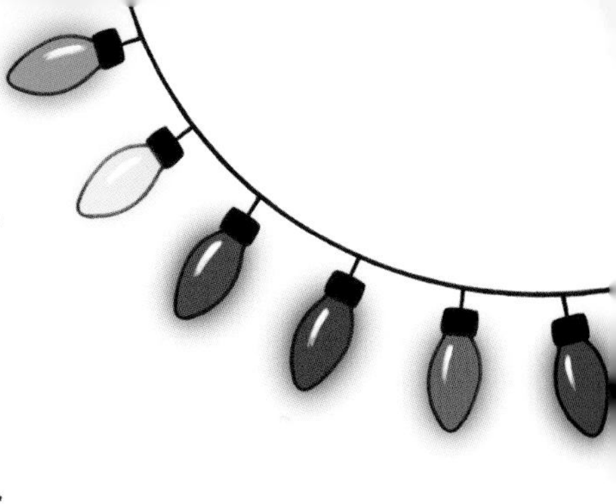

John 4:14

But whoever drinks the water I give will never be thirsty again. The water I give will become a spring of water flowing inside him. It will give him eternal life.

Romans 5:8

But Christ died for us while we were still sinners. In this way God shows his great love for us.

Romans 6:23

The payment for sin is death. But God gives us the free gift of life forever in Christ Jesus our Lord.

1 John 1:9

But if we confess our sins, he will forgive our sins. We can trust God. He does what is right. He will make us clean from all the wrongs we have done.

Bible Verses

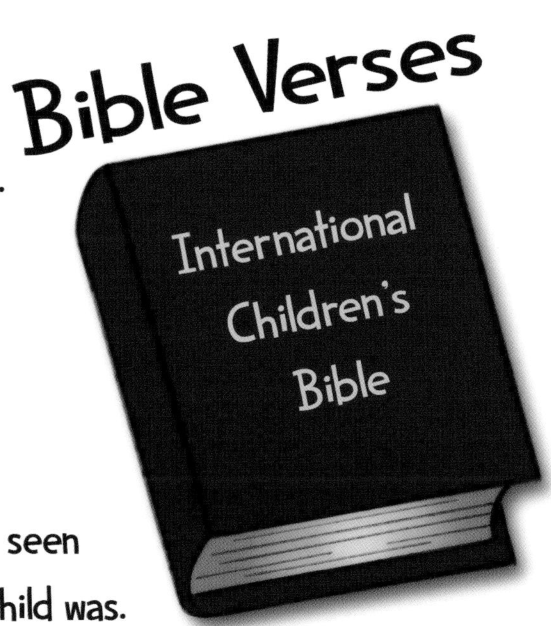

Psalms 51:7

Take away my sin, and I will be clean. Wash me, and I will be whiter than snow.

Luke 2:10

The angel said to them, "Don't be afraid, because I am bringing you some good news. It will be a joy to all the people."

Matthew 2:9

The wise men heard the king and then left. They saw the same star they had seen in the east. It went before them until it stopped above the place where the child was.

2 Peter 3:18

But grow in the grace and knowledge of our Lord and Savior Jesus Christ. Glory be to him now and forever! Amen.

Psalm 103:19

The Lord has set his throne in heaven. And his kingdom rules over everything.

Matthew 5:16

In the same way, you should be a light for other people. Live so that they will see the good things you do. Live so that they will praise your Father in heaven.

The Birth of Jesus

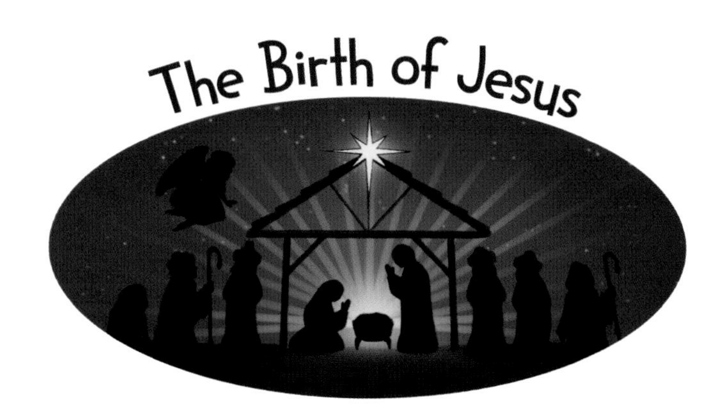

Luke 2: 1-20

At that time, Augustus Caesar sent an order to all people in the countries that were under Roman rule. The order said that they must list their names in a register. 2 This was the first registration taken while Quirinius was governor of Syria. 3 And everyone went to their own towns to be registered. 4 So Joseph left Nazareth, a town in Galilee. He went to the town of Bethlehem in Judea. This town was known as the town of David. Joseph went there because he was from the family of David. 5 Joseph registered with Mary because she was engaged to marry him. (Mary was now pregnant.) 6 While Joseph and Mary were in Bethlehem, the time came for her to have the baby. 7 She gave birth to her first son. There were no rooms left in the inn. So she wrapped the baby with cloths and laid him in a box where animals are fed.

Some Shepherds Hear About Jesus

8 That night, some shepherds were in the fields nearby watching their sheep. 9 An angel of the Lord stood before them. The glory of the Lord was shining around them, and suddenly they became very frightened. 10 The angel said to them, "Don't be afraid, because I am bringing you some good news. It will be a joy to all the people. 11 Today your Savior was born in David's town. He is Christ, the Lord. 12 This is how you will know him: You will find a baby wrapped in cloths and lying in a feeding box." 13 Then a very large group of angels from heaven joined the first angel. All the angels were praising God, saying:

14 "Give glory to God in heaven, and on earth let there be peace to the people who please God."

15 Then the angels left the shepherds and went back to heaven. The shepherds said to each other, "Let us go to Bethlehem and see this thing that has happened. We will see this thing the Lord told us about." 16 So the shepherds went quickly and found Mary and Joseph. 17 And the shepherds saw the baby lying in a feeding box. Then they told what the angels had said about this child. 18 Everyone was amazed when they heard what the shepherds said to them. 19 Mary hid these things in her heart; she continued to think about them. 20 Then the shepherds went back to their sheep, praising God and thanking him for everything that they had seen and heard. It was just as the angel had told them.

International Children's Bible version

Christmas Traditions

Learn more about the history of traditional decorations and then see if you can find them in the story!

The star that we top our tree with every Christmas represents the star of Bethlehem that guided the wise men to Jesus.

Christmas gifts represent the gifts the wise men gave to Jesus. The bow symbolizes unity and being tied to each other in service.

The Christmas tree is an evergreen and represents everlasting life. The needles of Christmas trees point toward heaven.

The Christmas wreath symbolizes eternity and endless hope. Wreaths are also a symbol of God's everlasting love having no beginning or end.

Christmas bells ring to symbolize an important message has been spread. At Christmas, it means our savior has been born.

Gingerbread Men remind us of God creating Adam in the Garden of Eden, signifying His creation of all of us.

Mistletoe only survives by attaching itself to a tree. To Christians, it represents how we only exist because of God's love.

Candy Canes have white to show purity and red to represent Jesus' sacrifice. The shape symbolizes the staff of the Good Shepherd.

Angels are part of Christmas to remind us of the angel who appeared to the shepherds. They symbolize God's presence and love.

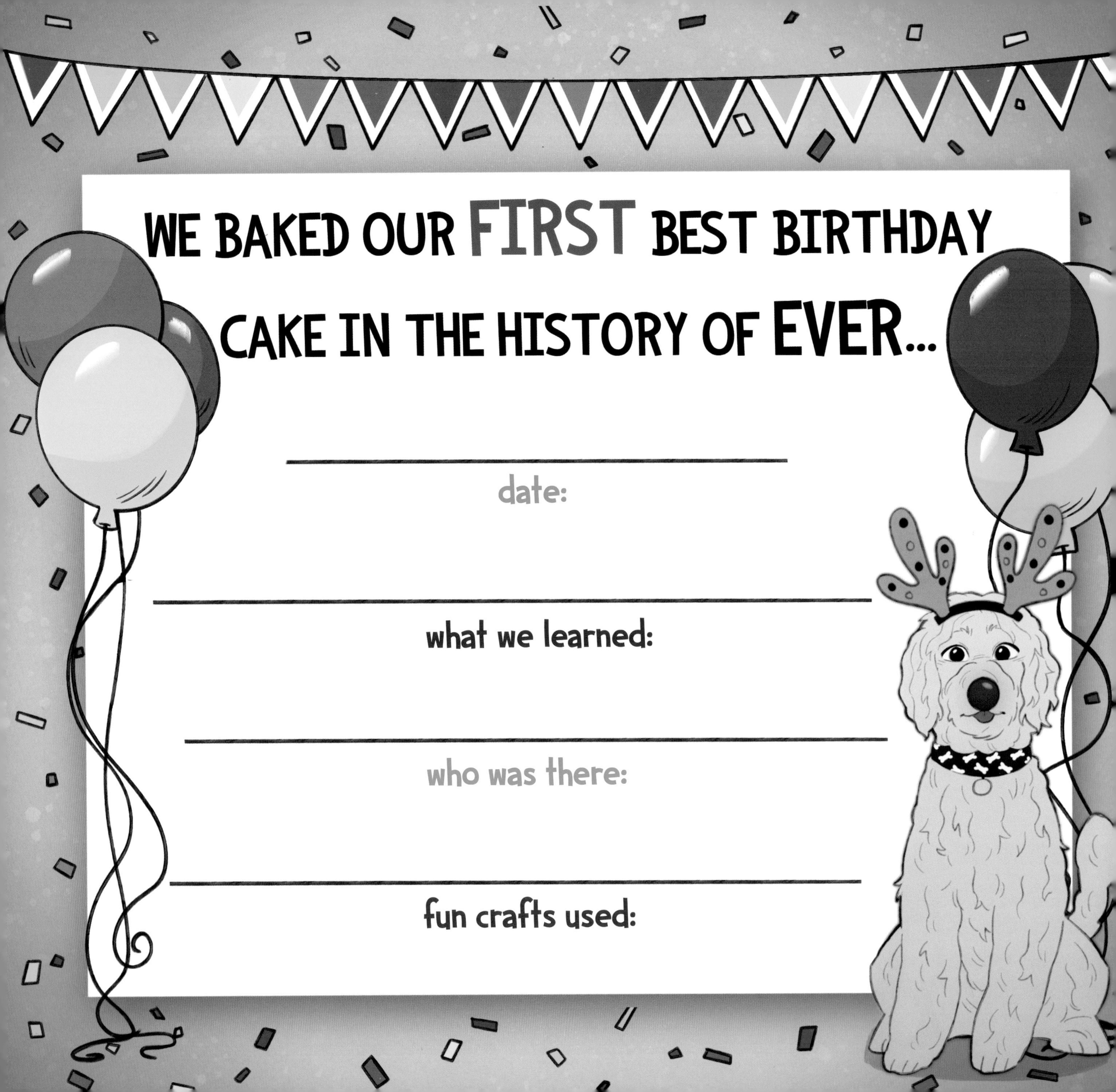
WE BAKED OUR FIRST BEST BIRTHDAY CAKE IN THE HISTORY OF EVER...
date:
what we learned:
who was there:
fun crafts used: